Wild and Beautiful

Written by Amanda Esch-Cormier
Illustrated by Naya Kirichenko
Copyright: 2021

Copyright © 2021 Amanda Esch-Cormier. Illustrations copyright © 2021 Naya Kirichenko. All rights reserved. No part of this book may be reproduced or transmitted in any form or by any means, electronic or mechanical, including photocopying, recording, or by any information storage and retrieval system, without written permission from the author. For information: amandaeschcormier@gmail.com

Printed in the United States

ISBN:9781737839309

To Hazel and Marley, my sweet wild ones.
Thank you for the great adventure of being
your mama.

When I was young,
I dreamed of a wild
and beautiful life.

I dreamed
of traveling to every
corner of the world.

I'd meet new people in cafes
and we'd discover
that we spoke the same
language of laughter.

I dreamed of climbing
tall mountains
and swimming in
oceans.

Of flying in planes
through big fluffy clouds.

Of dancing all night
to loud,
loud, loud music.

I'd sing on big stages,
to big roaring crowds.

Always ready to take on
the next adventure,
learn the next big thing.

There was nothing
I couldn't see or do.
Nothing was out of reach.

But then came you.

And even though
I've flown in the sky,
climbed mountains,
swam in oceans,

met thousands of people,
danced and sang my heart out,

and still do those things now:

There is nothing in my life
that compares to you.

You, my love,
are my wild and beautiful.

Now it's your turn,
my sweet wild one.

What will you dream
of doing with your
wild and beautiful life?

There is joy in the dreaming,
oh, the adventures you'll have!

Maybe
you'll grow a big garden
with flowers
that reach for the sky.

You could cruise into space, discovering new far away frontiers.

You could live on the top
of a mountain just to
enjoy morning sunrises
with the birds.

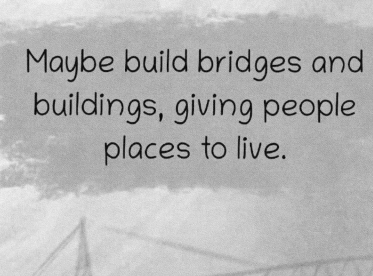

Maybe build bridges and
buildings, giving people
places to live.

What about being a doctor? Your bright mind could find a cure for anything.

Start a collection of beautiful paintings that fill your heart with wonder.

You master the art of baking. Days filled with cinnamon strudels and strawberry pies.

Or spend your time
showing love to the
people around you,
no matter who they are.

There is so much you can
do and so much to love
in the magical world.
I'll be here waiting to see
what you find.

Let's start the planning!
Your adventures await!

I can't wait to see what you,
my wild and beautiful one,
do with your days.

Made in United States
North Haven, CT
28 November 2022

27425783R00029